SUPER HEROES

WONDER WOMAN

TALES OF
PARADISE
ISLAND

JET-POWERED JUSTICE

BY
MICHAEL DAHL

ILLUSTRATED BY
O

WOND
WILLIAM

D1420252

34 4124 0016 0070

Raintree is an imprint of Capstone Global Library Limited, a
company incorporated in England and Wales having its
registered office at 264 Banbury Road, Oxford, OX2 7DY –
Registered company number: 6695582

www.raintree.co.uk
myorders@raintree.co.uk

Edited by Christopher Harbo
Designed by Brann Garvey
Originated by Capstone Global Library Ltd
Printed and bound in India

ISBN 978 1 4747 6407 0
22 21 20 19 18
10 9 8 7 6 5 4 3 2 1

British Library Cataloguing in Publication Data
A full catalogue record for this book is available from the British Library.

CONTENTS

INTRODUCTION..**4**

CHAPTER 1
GIANT JAM..**7**

CHAPTER 2
MAN OF METAL..**14**

CHAPTER 3
ANGRY ARES..**19**

CHAPTER 4
BRONZE BATTLE..**24**

CHAPTER 5
JET OF JUSTICE..**28**

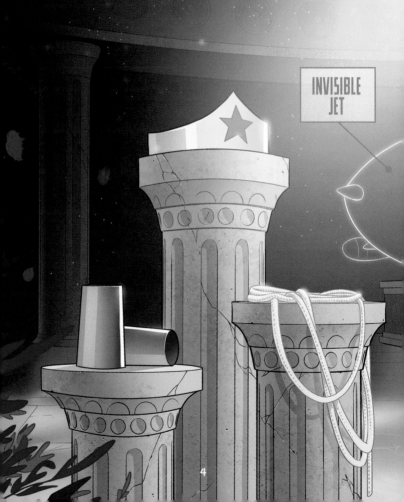

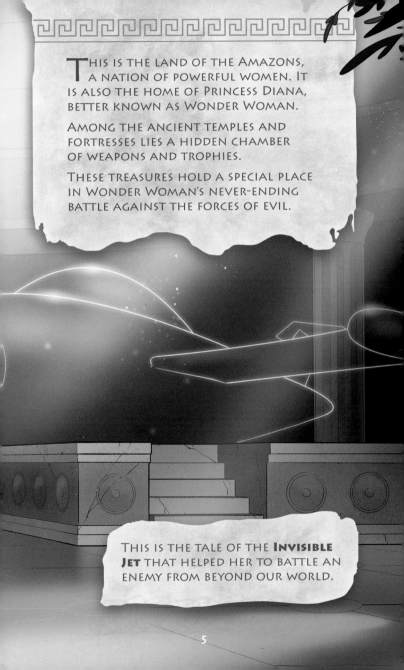

This is the land of the Amazons, a nation of powerful women. It is also the home of Princess Diana, better known as Wonder Woman.

Among the ancient temples and fortresses lies a hidden chamber of weapons and trophies.

These treasures hold a special place in Wonder Woman's never-ending battle against the forces of evil.

This is the tale of the **Invisible Jet** that helped her to battle an enemy from beyond our world.

CHAPTER 1

GIANT JAM

On a sunny afternoon, Wonder Woman enjoys a drive with her friend Steve Trevor. He is driving his sports car across the bridge that leads to Gateway City.

Wonder Woman closes her eyes and leans her head back.

The sun feels so good and warm, she thinks. *It's turning out to be a beautiful day!*

HONNNNK!
HONNNNK!

The car suddenly stops. Wonder Woman's eyes snap open.

"Steve, what's wrong?" Wonder Woman asks.

Steve stares through the windscreen with a frown.

"A giant traffic jam!" he says.

All the lanes of traffic leading into the city are blocked. Cars, trucks, buses and motorcycles are at a standstill.

Angry people honk their horns. A few drivers step out of their cars, looking towards the city.

Steve says, "I wonder how long it will–"

"Steve, look!" says Wonder Woman, cutting him off. She gets out of the sports car and looks towards the city.

AAAAAIIIIIEEEEEEE!

Several people on the bridge begin to scream. Off in the distance, a huge shadowy figure towers over the buildings.

"A giant!" says Wonder Woman.

"It can't be the villain Giganta," Steve says, shaking his head. "You captured her recently."

"I have to go," says Wonder Woman. She walks towards the edge of the bridge and thinks a silent command.

Come to me, she says in her mind.

VROOOOSSHHH!

Wonder Woman's Invisible Jet swoops out of the sky.

CHAPTER 2

MAN OF METAL

The Invisible Jet dives towards the bridge.

As it zooms closer, Wonder Woman leaps into the air. She flies over the parked cars and trucks.

Just as the jet dips below the bridge, Wonder Woman lands in the open cockpit.

ZHOOOOOOMMMM!

Wonder Woman steers the jet towards Gateway City.

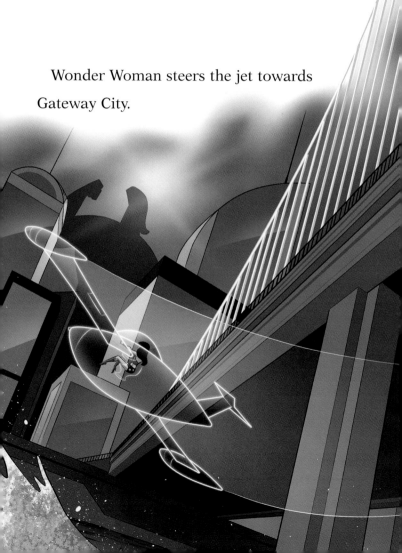

"I need to get a better look at that giant," Wonder Woman says to herself.

Zooming over the city's buildings, she sees the towering menace up close.

It is a gigantic warrior made of bronze.

The huge man lifts a massive bronze sword. Sunlight flashes off the blade. He slashes the sword towards the swooping jet.

SWIIISSSHHH!

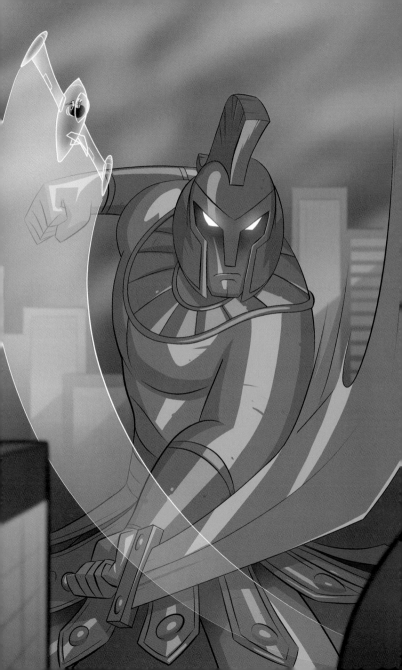

Wonder Woman guides the Invisible Jet swiftly past the deadly weapon.

WHOOOOSHHHHH!

This creature doesn't look man-made, thinks Wonder Woman. *Someone from Olympus must be behind this.*

CHAPTER 3

ANGRY ARES

An angry, dark cloud appears above the bronze giant.

A titanic helmet with glowing eyes rises from the swirling mist.

"Ares!" shouts Wonder Woman.

Ares, the God of War, looks down at the city.

"I see you've met Talos, my newest weapon," says Ares.

"Why have you left Olympus?" asks Wonder Woman.

"Humans are stupid creatures," the villain says. "They will think Talos was sent from another country. He will start another war!"

HA! HA! HA! HA! HA!

The God of War laughs. Bright lightning crashes from the swirling cloud.

"Soon the humans will call the military to help them," says Ares. "With more fighting and destruction, my power will grow stronger."

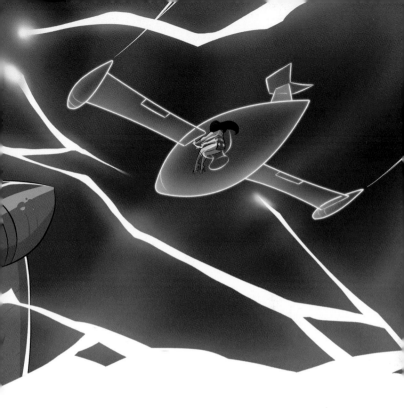

"Not if I can help it!" shouts Wonder Woman.

Ares laughs again and disappears.

Wonder Woman aims her jet towards the bronze giant.

CHAPTER 4

BRONZE BATTLE

Talos' massive feet crush empty police cars on the streets below.

As Wonder Woman closes in on the giant, she leaps out of her jet.

"This calls for hand-to-hand combat," Wonder Woman cries.

Wonder Woman grabs her golden lasso. She twirls the rope and then throws it at the giant.

The lasso captures Talos' fist as he swipes at a nearby news helicopter. The fist pulls the lasso and Wonder Woman along with it.

"My lasso's not working!" groans Wonder Woman. "It has no effect on him because he's made of metal. He's not human."

Wonder Woman hears the cries of people in the streets.

I need more power! she thinks.

CHAPTER 5

JET OF JUSTICE

Wonder Woman jumps back into her Invisible Jet. She buzzes round and round the rampaging giant.

"Perhaps I could zoom in a circle and wrap him up in a cable," she says to herself.

Talos marches along a busy street.

But if Talos falls, he could crush the citizens and police, Wonder Woman thinks.

Wonder Woman feels warmth on her face. Sunlight passes through the windscreen of the Invisible Jet.

"Heat!" she says to herself. "Of course!"

Wonder Woman zooms even closer to the bronze menace.

The giant's sword strikes at her again.

Wonder Woman pushes a button. Flames
flare from the Invisible Jet's engines.

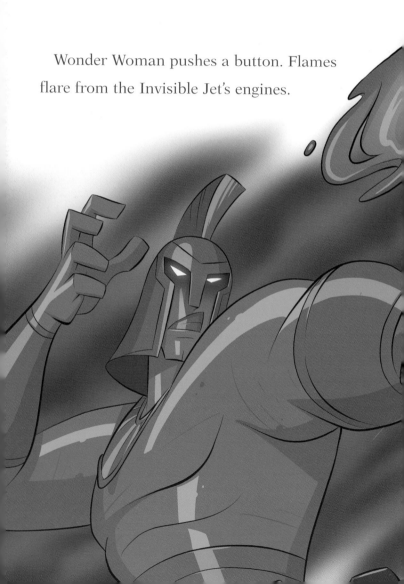

The high heat melts the giant's bronze blade.

"You're just metal, Talos!" shouts Wonder Woman. "And my jet can withstand super hot temperatures."

The swift jet sweeps past Talos' bronze helmet. The helmet begins to melt. Liquid metal covers the giant's face and blinds him.

Again and again, the jet skims across the giant's body. Talos melts and sinks slowly, and safely, into the street.

"Looks like Talos couldn't handle the heat!" says Wonder Woman.

Ares' voice booms out from the dark cloud above the city.

"You've won this time, Wonder Woman," he says. "But I'll be back!"

The angry cloud dissolves in the sunlight as the Invisible Jet soars back to the busy bridge.

GLOSSARY

bronze metal made of copper and tin; bronze has a gold-brown colour

citizens people who live in a particular town or city

cockpit area in the front of a plane where the pilot sits

combat fighting between people or armies

menace someone who is a threat or danger to others

military armed forces of a state or country

Olympus home of the gods in Greek mythology

titanic huge

villain wicked or evil character in a story

DISCUSS

1. Wonder Woman uses her mind to call her Invisible Jet. Imagine if you could control things with your mind. What would you control and why?

2. How do the illustrations for this story get across the idea that Wonder Woman's jet is invisible? In what other ways could the artwork show something that can't be seen?

3. Wonder Woman uses heat to melt the metal giant. What other ways could she have used to defeat it?

WRITE

1. Imagine if you could create a giant like Talos. What would your giant be and what would you do with it? Write a short story about your giant's adventures.

2. Ares comes from Olympus, home of the Greek gods. Write a paragraph describing what you think Olympus looks like and draw a picture of it.

3. Wonder Woman defeats Ares at the end of the story. But the God of War says he'll be back. Write a short story where Ares returns and Wonder Woman must face him again.

AUTHOR

Michael Dahl is the author of more than 200 books for children and young adults, including *Bedtime for Batman*, *Be A Star, Wonder Woman!* and *Sweet Dreams, Supergirl*. He has won the AEP Distinguished Achievement Award three times for his non-fiction, a Teachers' Choice Award from *Learning* magazine and a Seal of Excellence from the Creative Child Awards. He is also the author of the Batman Tales of the Batcave and Superman Tales of the Fortress of Solitude series. Dahl currently lives in Minnesota, USA.

ILLUSTRATOR

Omar Lozano lives in Monterrey, Mexico. He has always been crazy about illustration and is constantly on the lookout for awesome things to draw. In his free time, he watches lots of films, reads fantasy and sci-fi books, and draws! Omar has worked for Marvel, DC, IDW, Capstone and several other publishers.